專門替中國人寫的英文課本

初級本（上冊）

序

李家同

我小的時候，就不怕唸英文，我總覺得物理還有可能使我感到困惑，英文呢？我就搞不清楚英文有什麼難的，只要將生字查一下，就懂得句子的意思了。至於寫英文作文，我也從來不覺得有什麼了不起的，我當然比不上那些洋人，但我很少犯嚴重的文法錯誤。

後來我自己做起國中生的英文義務家教了，我忽然發現一般的國中生認為唸英文是很麻煩的事，英文的生字很多，不容易記，英文文法尤其對一般人不利，動詞的時態常令人頭痛。我總記得，有一次我的學生問我，如何將以下的句子換成被動語氣：

Have you ever read this book?

我完全傻了眼，我花了好多時間才把這個講清楚。

我的女兒在小學裡沒有學過一個英文字，進國中一年級，從A,B,C學起，我想她一定完蛋了，一定會來求我幫她的忙，可是她沒有來找我，她和我一樣，有時會被數學或者自然的難題難倒，可是，英文好像從來就不是問題。

我終於想通了，英文對一般中國人是很難的，我對英文沒有問題，絕非我聰明，而是因為我的爸爸媽媽都會講英文，我有什麼問題，問問他們就可以了。我到現在都還記得我的爸爸教我現在完成式是怎麼回事，我的女兒情形相同，她的爸爸媽媽又是會英文的人，有了這種環境，學英文就不難了。

如果家人沒有人會講英文，但有家教來教，或者有財力去進補習班，英文又不難了。

過去，我們國家的小學不教英文，國中英文教科書是國立編譯館編的，我

用這種教科書教當時的國中生，倒還可以應付，學生也勉強可以接受。在我擔任靜宜大學校長的時候，就有一位美國神父常來找我，他一再地說我國的英文教科書太難了，他的理由非常簡單，他說如果美國國中學這麼難的中文，美國的國中生早就造反了。我一直敷衍這位好心的神父，因為我覺得我用那本國立編譯館的英文教科書，還沒有太大的問題。

忽然之間，我的問題來了，我們的教科書不再由國立編譯館編，而是由民間的出版商來編，我教的一位國中一年級學生給我看他的英文教科書，這本書的生字奇難無比，我也去看了一下其他的版本，也都一樣。

從此以後，我就開始好好地想我們國家的英文入門教科書有什麼樣的問題，我想了很久，發現至少**我們的入門教科書有以下幾個缺點：**

1. 我們的英文教科書一律沒有中文說明，連入門的都是如此，也難怪我們的學生覺得學英文好難。試想，假如我們教英國人中文，入門的教科書裡沒有一句英文，試問那些學生如何能懂？

我和一位在大學教英文的教授聊到這點，他也完全同意，他說他想學法文，卻不得其門而入。虧得他運氣好，找到一個網站，這個網站上以英文來解釋法文，他大喜過望，也有了安全感，從此就不再怕法文了。

2. 我們的教科書號稱是包含了英文文法的，但是英文文法談何容易。舉個例子來說，對我們中國人來說，你是、他是、我是、小貓是，任何名詞後面都用同樣的「是」，英文就不同了。I am, You are, He is, They are 等等都不同，這還是現在式，到了過去式，事情就要更加糟了，而且這些文法上的規矩都是沒有道理的，我實在無法告訴學生，為什麼 I 的後面要跟 am，在我看來，全部都用 be，不是很好嗎？

對於初學者而言，he 要用 has，不可以用 have，也是十分麻煩的。

我們的英文教科書，對於這些文法，一概不解釋，因為他們無法解釋，如果他們用中文解釋，乃是犯了大忌，我國的英文教科書裡是不可以用中文的。用英文解釋，那又更不可能，因為小孩子初學英文，如何能看懂英文的解釋

呢？

　　所以我們同學的英文文法基本觀念只好由老師來決定，如果老師教得好，學生就不會犯錯，否則同學就錯誤百出。

　　3. 書中的練習太少了。

　　英文這種東西，是沒有什麼深奧的，只要反覆練習，就一定學得會，一般英文教科書的練習都寥寥可數。學生沒有什麼練習的機會。

　　我實在希望能有一套英文入門教科書，將以上的缺點一一改過來，也就是說，這本書至少應該有以下幾個特色：

　　1. 書中必須有中文翻譯，不僅英文生字有中文解釋，英文句子也要有中文的翻譯，而且也要用中文來解釋。舉例來說，第三人稱，現在式，單數時，動詞要加s，一般的英文教科書並沒有提到，更從不強調，一旦書中有中文解釋，問題就解決了，我們總可以用中文將這個規則說清楚，講明白。

　　2. 書中必須要有中翻英，在過去，中翻英好像是禁忌，那些偉大的學者一再強調，說我們在寫英文句子的時候，必須忘記中文，這種想法，基本假設是我們有一個說英文的環境，大家都只講英文，不講任何其他語言，這樣我們當然就可以用英文的思維方式來寫英文句子。

　　可是，我們沒有這種環境，我們平時都講中文，怎麼可能不從中文想起？中翻英仍然是非常重要的。因為我們都是用中文想的。

　　根據我的經驗，任何一個小孩子，只要他會翻譯一些中文的句子，他就會有好的成就感，大家不要以為「我是一個男孩子」和「他不喜歡我」，這類句子太簡單，其實不然，如果小孩子會出口成章地將這些中文句子正確地譯成英文，他一定會感到十分快樂了。很多初學英文的孩子，會說 "He don't like me."

　　3. 每一課都要非常簡單，舉例來說，否定的句子有兩種，一種是 verb to be 的否定句，另一種是一般動詞的否定，前者可以直接改成否定句，後者必須加一個 do 動詞，兩者截然不同，入門的教科書應該將這兩種不同的情形分

開來講，讀這本書的人可以循序漸進，慢慢地來，弄懂了一些，再看下一課。

　　4. 這本書必須不要太貴，所以編排不要太昂貴，越簡單越好，絕對不要有圖畫，更不要有彩色，因為我的心目中有很多家境不太好的孩子，他們根本沒有能力買貴的書。

　　5. 這本書必須有一個光碟，專門用來訓練發音之用，對於英文初學者，最恐怖的事是不會發音。假如有一個孩子在上課時沒有學會唸一些字，回家又沒有人可以教，他就完全垮掉了。至於學音標，我擔心對初學者是二度傷害，因為英文字母已經很難了，還要認音標，豈不是難上加難？

　　我現在終於有這兩本入門的書了，文老師寫的書簡單又容易讀，有很多練習，包含中翻英，應該是入門的好書。

　　我想這兩本書不可能成為學校的正式教科書的，但是這些書卻適合於任何一個初步入門的人，不論老幼。很多老年人，當年沒有學好英文，仍可以用這兩本書作為入門之用。

　　我在此要給每一位用這本書的老師一個建議：不要趕進度，慢慢來。一再地反覆練習，直到你的學生非常熟悉為止。

　　我已經用這本書教幾位小朋友了，一開始，我請他們翻譯「我是一個男孩」，他們還結結巴巴說不清楚，過了一陣子，再問他們這種句子，他們會嫌煩，因為他們已經熟得不得了，前些日子，我請他們翻譯「他不是我的老師」，他們也都能順口而出，我高興，他們也高興。昨天，他們會翻譯「他每天上學」這類的句子，而且也會在動詞後面加 S，我正在準備教「他不是每天上學」這種句子。

　　這兩本書也都有了光碟作伴，如果你不認識書中的字，可以點一下，就會聽到這個字的發音，光碟也有聽寫的功能。希望老師們能夠幫助孩子們利用光碟。

　　總而言之，我希望很多家中沒有人會講英文的孩子們，以後不會太怕英文，至少這本書裡面都是中文的解釋，應該不至於是天書了。

目次

字母表

Aa	Bb	Cc	Dd	Ee
Ff	Gg	Hh	Ii	Jj
Kk	Ll	Mm	Nn	Oo
Pp	Qq	Rr	Ss	Tt
Uu	Vv	Ww	Xx	Yy
Zz				

第一課 （朗讀光碟 第 2 軌）

家人

我們常常要和家人談話，因此我們在第一課，
先學一些與家人有關的英文字。

1-1　生字

father	爸爸 簡稱為 Dad
mother	媽媽 簡稱為 Mom
son	兒子
daughter	女兒
brother	哥哥、弟弟
sister	姊姊、妹妹
boy	男孩
girl	女孩
and	和
a	一個

1-2 課文

a mother and a father（ a Mom and a Dad ）
一個媽媽和一個爸爸

a daughter and a son
一個女兒和一個兒子

a brother and a sister
一個哥哥和一個妹妹

a boy and a girl
一個男孩和一個女孩

1-3　練習題

1-3-1　選選看

1. （　　）哥哥（1）son　（2）father　（3）brother
2. （　　）媽媽（1）father　（2）mother　（3）brother
3. （　　）妹妹（1）sister　（2）girl　（3）mother
4. （　　）女孩（1）brother　（2）sister　（3）girl
5. （　　）爸爸（1）father　（2）brother　（4）boy
6. （　　）姊姊（1）girl　（2）sister　（3）mother
7. （　　）弟弟（1）brother　（2）boy　（3）father
8. （　　）男孩（1）sister　（2）boy　（3）brother

1-3-2　下面的字，英文該怎麼寫：

1. 男孩 _____
2. 哥哥 _____
3. 妹妹 _____
4. 爸爸 _____
5. 弟弟 _____
6. 姊姊 _____
7. 媽媽 _____
8. 女孩 _____
9. 一個媽媽和一個爸爸

　　_____

10.　一個姊姊和一個哥哥

　　　_____

11.　一個女兒和一個兒子

　　　_____

12.　一個媽媽和一個姊姊

　　　_____

13.　一個爸爸和一個妹妹

　　　_____

14.　一個弟弟和一個姊姊

　　　_____

15.　一個女孩和一個男孩

　　　_____

第二課

（朗讀光碟 第 3 軌）

你、我、他

我們說話的時候，總要提到你、我、他三種稱呼。我們現在將這些字寫在下面，請注意：英文中的「他」有男的「他」（he），有女的「她」（she），還有動物的「牠」（it）和沒有生命的「它」（it）。

2-1　生字

I	我
you	你
he	他
she	她
it	牠、它
we	我們
you	你們
they	他們
am, is, are	是
dog	狗
cat	貓
friend	朋友

2-2　課文

I am a boy.	我是一個男孩。
You are a girl.	妳是一個女孩。
She is a girl.	她是一個女孩。
He is a boy.	他是一個男孩。
It is a cat.	牠是一隻貓。
We are friends.	我們都是朋友。
You are girls.	妳們都是女孩。
They are brothers and sisters.	
	他們是兄弟姊妹。
They are dogs.	牠們都是狗。

＊ you 可以當成「你」或「你們」或「妳」、「妳們」。

＊ They 可以當成「牠們」「她們」「他們」，還有沒有生命的「它們」。

＊你們有沒有注意到名詞單數時不加 "s"，如 a boy；多數時，要加 "s"，如 boys 和 girls。

 2-2-1

各位會發現英文中的「是」比我們中文的「是」複雜多了。

I am

You are

He is

She is

It is

We are

You are

They are

2-2-2　請看下列圖表：

I	am
You	are
He	
She	is
It	
We	
You	are
They	

2-2-3 簡寫

I am 可以簡寫為 I'm
You are 可以簡寫為 You're
He is 可以簡寫為 He's
She is 可以簡寫為 She's
It is 可以簡寫為 It's
We are 可以簡寫為 We're
You are 可以簡寫為 You're
They are 可以簡寫為 They're

 2-2-4 請看下列例句：

1. I'm a girl.
2. You're a boy.
3. She's a girl.
4. He's a boy.
5. It's a cat.
6. We're brothers.
7. You're sisters.
8. They're mother and daughter.

＊ 凡是句子的開始，第一個字母都要大寫，每一句寫完後還要加一點「.」當成句點。

2-3 練習題

2-3-1 填填看

1. I _____ a boy.

2. It _____ a cat.

3. He _____ a boy.

4. She _____ a girl.

5. You _____ a boy.

6. You _____ boys.

7. They _____ girls.

8. We _____ boys.

9. They _____ friends.

10. They _____ brothers.

11. You _____ friends.

12. We _____ brother and sister.

13. You _____ father and son.

14. They _____ girls and boys.

15. They _____ dogs and cats.

2-3-2 英文該怎麼寫?

1. 我們是朋友。

   _____

2. 他是哥哥。

   _____

3.　我是妹妹。
　　_____

4.　他們是兄妹。
　　_____

5.　他是爸爸。
　　_____

6.　他是兒子。
　　_____

7.　他們是父子。
　　_____

8.　她是媽媽。
　　_____

9.　我是女兒。
　　_____

10.　我們是母女。
　　_____

11.　她是姊姊。
　　_____

12.　妳們是姊妹。
　　_____

13.　牠們是一隻狗和一隻貓。
　　_____

14.　他們是男孩和女孩。
　　_____

15.　妳們是女兒。
　　_____

第三課　　（朗讀光碟　第4軌）

有

我們常用英文表示我「有」什麼東西，表示「有」有兩種形式：have 和 has。什麼時候用 have？什麼時候用 has？請先猜猜看。

3-1　生字

have , has	有
many	很多
student	學生
teacher	老師
book	書
house	房子
chair	椅子
desk	桌子

I have a son.	我有一個兒子。
You have a desk and many chairs.	你有一張桌子和許多椅子。
He has many students.	他有很多學生。
She has a sister.	她有一個姊姊。
It has many friends.	牠有很多朋友。
You have many daughters.	你們有很多女兒。
We have a dog.	我們有一隻狗。
They have many cats.	他們有很多隻貓。

3-2-1 請看下列圖表：

I		
You	have	a house.
She		
He	has	a house.
It		
We		
You	have	a house.
They		

* 猜到 have 和 has 的差別了沒？

  請注意：除了第三人稱 she, he, it 用 has 外，其他都用 have。

* be 動詞不可以跟動詞 have 連在一起：

  I am have a house.（錯）

  She is have a dog. （錯）

  She has a dog. （對）

  I have a cat.（對）

3-3　練習題

3-3-1　選選看

（請注意：有的動詞用「是」，有的用「有」。）

1. （　　）I （1）have （2）am （3）is （4）has　many books.
2. （　　）She （1）have （2）am （3）are （4）has　a mother.
3. （　　）He （1）have （2）am （3）is （4）are　a teacher.
4. （　　）They （1）are （2）am （3）is （4）has　cats.
5. （　　）You （1）have （2）am （3）is （4）has　many brothers.
6. （　　）It （1）have （2）am （3）is （4）are　a dog.
7. （　　）We （1）have （2）am （3）is （4）are　teachers.
8. （　　）They （1）have （2）am （3）is （4）has　many houses.
9. （　　）You （1）has （2）am （3）is （4）are　a student.
10. （　　）She （1）has （2）am （3）have （4）are　many dogs.

3-3-2　填填看

（請注意：有的動詞用「是」，有的用「有」。）

1. I ＿＿＿＿＿＿＿ a dog. （我有一條狗）
2. She ＿＿＿＿＿＿＿ many brothers. （她有很多哥哥）
3. You ＿＿＿＿＿＿＿ a house. （你有一幢房子）
4. They ＿＿＿＿＿＿＿ brothers. （他們是兄弟）
5. We ＿＿＿＿＿＿＿ a cat. （我們有一隻貓）
6. He ＿＿＿＿＿＿＿ many sisters. （他有很多妹妹）
7. It ＿＿＿＿＿＿ a dog. （牠是一條狗）

8.　They ＿＿＿＿＿＿＿＿＿ boys and girls（他們是男孩和女孩）

9.　We ＿＿＿＿＿＿＿＿ a daughter.（我們有一個女兒）

10.　They ＿＿＿＿＿＿＿ many sons.（他們有很多個兒子）

11.　We ＿＿＿＿＿＿ sisters.（我們是姊妹）

12.　He ＿＿＿＿＿＿ many chairs.（他有很多張椅子）

13.　They ＿＿＿＿＿＿ cats.（牠們是貓）

14.　I ＿＿＿＿＿＿ dogs and cats.（我有狗和貓）

15.　They ＿＿＿＿＿＿a daughter.（他們有一個女兒）

16.　She ＿＿＿＿＿＿＿ many students.（她有許多學生。）

17.　I ＿＿＿＿＿＿ many books.（我有很多書。）

18.　We ＿＿＿＿＿ teachers.（我們是老師。）

19.　They ＿＿＿＿＿＿ students.（他們是學生。）

20.　You ＿＿＿＿＿＿ many brothers.（你有好多兄弟。）

3-3-3　改錯

1.　I has（have）a book.

2.　You has many cats.

3.　She have a book.

4.　They has many sons.

5.　We has many chairs.

6.　It have a house.

7.　You has many books.

8.　I has many brothers and sisters.

9.　He have cats and dogs.

10.　She have many desks.

11.　They are have many friends.

12.　We have many cat.

13.　It is book.

14.　We are have a cat.

15.　She is has many books.

第四課

（朗讀光碟 第 5 軌）

數字

日常生活裡常常要用到一些數字，我們來看 0 到 10 的英文該怎麼說。

4-1　生字

zero	（0）
one	（1）
two	（2）
three	（3）
four	（4）
five	（5）
six	（6）
seven	（7）
eight	（8）
nine	（9）
ten	（10）

4-2　課文

one cat	一隻貓
two dogs	兩隻狗
three boys	三個男孩
four girls	四個女孩
five students	五個學生
six teachers	六個老師
seven books	七本書
eight houses	八幢房子
nine chairs	九張椅子
ten desks	十張桌子

＊記得嗎？多數要加 s

4-2-1　現在把次序打亂，你能填得出正確的數字來嗎？

three（　　）, two（　　）, five（　　）, zero（　　）, seven（　　）, ten（　　）,
one（　　）, four（　　）, six（　　）, eight（　　）, nine（　　）

4-3　練習題

4-3-1　選選看

1. （　　）three dogs（1）三隻狗（2）九隻狗（3）五隻狗

2. （　　）five cats（1）十隻貓（2）五隻貓（3）六隻貓

3. （　　）ten students（1）七個學生（2）兩個學生（3）十個學生

4. （　　）four daughters（1）四個女兒（2）七個女兒（3）三個女兒

5. （　　）eight chairs（1）兩張椅子（2）八張椅子（3）十張椅子

6. （　　）seven houses（1）四幢房子（2）七幢房子（3）六幢房子

7. （　　）six desks（1）六張桌子（2）三張桌子（3）九張桌子

8. （　　）one girl（1）兩個女孩（2）一個女孩（3）五個女孩

9. （　　）nine boys（1）九個男孩（2）七個男孩（3）八個男孩

10. （　　）ten friends（1）四個朋友（2）十個朋友（3）一個朋友

11. （　　）two sisters（1）兩姊妹（2）三姊妹（3）四姊妹

12. （　　）five brothers and sisters（1）三兄妹（2）九兄妹（3）五兄妹

13. （　　）three daughters（1）三個女兒（2）十個女兒（3）七個女兒

14. （　　）six friends（1）三個朋友（2）六個朋友（3）四個朋友

15. （　　）ten cats（1）十隻貓（2）九隻貓（3）五隻貓

4-3-2　填填看

1. 五個男孩 _____

2. 七個女孩 _____

3. 三個兒子 _____

4. 八張桌子 _____

5. 一個哥哥 _____

6. 六本書 _____

7. 兩個妹妹 _____

8. 四隻貓 _____

9. 十張椅子 _____

10. 九隻狗 _____

11. 五姊妹 _____

12. 兩個老師 _____

13. 一個女兒 _____

14. 三隻狗 _____

15. 八幢房子 _____

4-3-3 英文該怎麼寫？

1. 我有五隻貓。

    _____

2. 他有三隻狗。

    _____

3. 我們有四把椅子。

    _____

4. 他們有一張桌子。

    _____

5. 她有兩幢房子。

    _____

6. 我有十個學生。

    _____

7. 他有很多書。

_____

8. 你有三個朋友。

_____

9. 你們有兩位老師。

_____

10. 我們有九張椅子。

_____

第五課 （朗讀光碟 第6軌）

所有格
「我的、你的、他的」

在日常生活中，我們常常指出東西屬於「你的」、「我的」、或是「他的」，這些「你的」、「我的」、「他的」英文該怎麼說呢？

5-1　　生字

my	我的
your	你的
his	他的
her	她的
its	它的（牠的）
our	我們的
your	你們的
their	他們的

5-2　課文

She's my mom.	她是我的媽媽。
They're your daughters.	她們是你的女兒。
We're his mom and dad.	我們是他的爸媽。
You're her sisters.	妳們都是她的姊姊。
He's your teacher.	他是你們的老師。
They're our students.	他們是我們的學生。
She's their sister.	她是他們的妹妹。
My brother has a cat.	我哥哥有一隻貓。
Your sister has many students.	你的姊姊有很多學生。
Its house is big.	牠的房子大。
Your daughter has three dogs.	你們的女兒有三隻狗。
Our teacher has many students.	我們的老師有很多學生。
Their dad has many books.	他們的爸爸有很多書。

＊你還記得嗎？

I'm = I am, You're = You are, She's = She is, He's = He is,

It's = It is, We're = We are, You're = You are, They're = They are

5-2-1

如果要說「某某人的……」單數就用 "'s"

例如：一位老師的 a teacher's ，多數則用 "s'"

例如：老師們的 teachers'

Amy's cat	愛咪的貓 （Amy 是女人的名字）
my brother's books	我哥哥的書
students' chairs	學生們的椅子
my teachers' cars	我老師們的車
his mom's house	他媽媽的房子

5-2-2 請看圖表：

my 我的	book
your 你的	chair
his 他的	desk
her 她的	dog
its 牠的	house
your 你們的	sister
their 他們的	mom
our 我們的	dad
Amy's 愛咪的	daughter

＊ 注意：

It's a dog. （牠是一隻狗。）

It's → It is （牠是）

Its house is big.

（牠的房子很大。）

Its → （牠的）

It's 和 Its 不同，請不要弄錯。

5-3　　　　　練習題

5-3-1　填填看：

1.　＿＿＿＿＿＿＿ mother has a dog.

（他的媽媽有一條狗。）

2.　＿＿＿＿＿＿＿ brother has a house.

（她的哥哥有一幢房子。）

3.　＿＿＿＿＿＿＿ sisters have cars.

（我的姊妹都有車。）

4.　＿＿＿＿＿＿＿ brother has a daughter.

（他的哥哥有一個女兒。）

5.　＿＿＿＿＿＿＿ father has a sister.

（他們的爸爸有一個姊姊。）

6.　＿＿＿＿＿＿＿ dad has a car.

（你的爸爸有一輛車。）

7.　＿＿＿＿＿＿＿ brother has ten books.

（我的弟弟有十本書。）

8.　＿＿＿＿＿＿＿ mother has two houses.

（他的媽媽有兩幢房子。）

9.　＿＿＿＿＿＿＿ sister has three birds.

（我們的妹妹有三隻鳥。）

10.　＿＿＿＿＿＿＿ brothers have three dogs.

（他們的哥哥有三隻狗。）

11.　＿＿＿＿＿＿＿ brothers have four houses.

（我的哥哥們有四幢房子。）

12. _____ teacher _____ ten students.

（我的老師有十個學生。）

13. _____ students _____ dogs.

（他們的學生有狗。）

14. _____ friends _____ three cats.

（他們的朋友有三隻貓。）

15. _____ daughter _____ many books.

（他的女兒有很多書。）

5-3-2 改錯

1. His mother have（has）three daughters.

2. My sister are a student.

3. Her brothers is teachers.

4. My dad have three houses.

5. Their mom and dad has three sons.

6. Our brothers and sisters is students.

7. Your cats is have a house.

8. His sister are my friend.

9. Her son is has five cats.

10. Our teacher have a son.

11. Your brothers and sisters has two houses.

12. My brother has ten book.

13. Her mom is teacher.

14. His dad have a dog.

15. Their teachers are have books.

5-3-3 英文該怎麼寫？

（英文裡的「是」和「有」很容易混淆，請做下面的題目，看看你是否真的瞭解「是」和「有」的用法。）

1.　我是他的學生。

　　_____

2.　他是我的爸爸。

　　_____

3.　Amy 是我的妹妹。

　　_____

4.　Amy 有一個妹妹。

　　_____

5.　我的老師有三隻狗。

　　_____

6.　她的朋友有很多貓。

　　_____

7.　他們是我的學生。

　　_____

8.　他有很多學生。

　　_____

9.　我的女兒有很多書。

　　_____

10.　他們的兒子是我的朋友。

　　_____

第六課 （朗讀光碟 第 7 軌）

肯定和否定
（是、不是）

我們說話的時候，有時候用肯定的口氣，有時則用否定的口氣。肯定與否定的句型有些不同，本課將比較 be 動詞（am, is, are）的肯定和否定句的不同。be 動詞的否定很簡單，只要在 be 動詞後面加 not 就變成「不是」的意思了。

6-1　生字

am not　　　　　　不是

is not → isn't　　　不是

are not → aren't　　不是

singer　　　　　　歌星

actor　　　　　　演員

doctor　　　　　　醫生

nurse　　　　　　護士

pen　　　　　　　筆

pencil　　　　　　鉛筆

＊ am not 不能簡寫為amn't

6-2　課文

I am not a singer.	我不是歌星。
I'm an actor.	我是一個演員。

（英文發音有五個母音：a, e, i, o, u，母音前面的a〔一個〕要改為 an）。

She isn't a nurse.	她不是護士。
She is a doctor.	她是一個醫生。
It isn't a pen.	它不是枝筆。
It is a pencil.	它是枝鉛筆。
We aren't sisters.	我們不是姊妹。
We are mother and daughter.	我們是母女。
They aren't students.	他們不是學生。
They are teachers.	他們是老師。

 6-2-1

請看圖表你會更清楚 be 動詞（是、不是）否定句的用法：

I	am not	a student.學生
You	are not（aren't）	a teacher.老師
It	is not（isn't）	a pencil.鉛筆
She	is not（isn't）	a nurse.護士
He	is not（isn't）	a doctor.醫生
We	are not（aren't）	students.學生
You	are not（aren't）	singers.歌星
They	are not（aren't）	actors.演員

6-3 練習題

6-3-1 填充（請決定用 am not, isn't 還是 aren't）

1. I _____ an actor.

2. She _____ my teacher.

3. He _____ a doctor.

4. They _____ my sisters.

5. It _____ his dog.

6. We _____ nurses.

7. They _____my friends.

8. We _____his students.

9. You _____a singer.

10. He _____ a doctor.

11. She _____ his mom.

12. They _____ your pens.

13. I _____ his daughter.

14. You _____ nurses.

15. We _____ doctors.

16. He _____ a singer.

17. It _____ your pencil.

18. She _____ his student.

19. It _____ our house.

20. We _____ his sisters.

21. They _____ our chairs.

22.   She _____ my doctor.

23.   He _____ my brother's teacher.

24.   We _____ his brothers.

25.   He _____ my father.

6-3-2 改錯

1.He isn't my teachers.

2.They isn't my friends.

3.She aren't my daughter's friend.

4.Amy aren't his student.

5.My son isn't their friends.

6.The doctor's sons are my student.

7.We aren't his father's friend.

8.Her daughter aren't a nurse.

9.It is their dogs.

10.His daughters isn't doctors.

11.Our mom aren't his teacher.

12.Their son isn't our teachers.

13.My son isn't actor.

14.It isn't pencil.

15.They are pen.

6-3-3 英文該怎麼寫？

1.   他不是我媽媽的學生。

_____

2.　我們不是她的女兒。（daughter 記得要加 s）

_____

3.　牠不是她的狗。

_____

4.　它不是我的椅子。

_____

5.　你們不是我的學生。

_____

6.　我們不是她的老師。

_____

7.　牠不是我的貓。

_____

8.　Amy 不是我的女兒。

_____

9.　我們不是他們的朋友。

_____

10.　它們不是我們的桌子和椅子。（desks and chairs）

_____

第七課　　（朗讀光碟 第 8 軌）

肯定和否定
（有、沒有）

我們學完了 be 動詞肯定與否定的用法，現在看看動詞 have/has（有）的肯定與否定用法有何不同。 have/has 是動詞，否定時要在 have 前面加 do not 或 does not。

例如：I <u>do not</u> <u>have</u> sisters. She <u>does not</u> <u>have</u> brothers.

7-1　生字

do

do not→ don't（用在 I, you, we, they）

does

does not→ doesn't　（用在 he, she, it）

car　　　　　　　車

bicycle　　　　　腳踏車（簡稱為 bike）

bird　　　　　　鳥

computer　　　　電腦

milk　　　　　　牛奶

water　　　　　　水

table　　　　　　桌子（desk 是有抽屜的書桌）

7-2　課文

I don't have a car. I have a bicycle.

我沒有一輛車。我有一輛腳踏車。

You don't have a dog. You have a bird.

你沒有一隻狗。你有一隻鳥。

She doesn't have a computer. She has books.

她沒有一台電腦。她有書。

It doesn't have milk. It has water.

牠沒有牛奶。牠有水。

He doesn't have a house. He has a chair.

他沒有房子。他有一張椅子。

We don't have pencils. We have pens.

我們沒有鉛筆。我們有筆。

You don't have a table. You have many chairs.

你們沒有桌子。你們有很多椅子。

They don't have doctors. They have nurses.

他們沒有醫生。他們有護士。

7-3 請看下表，你會更清楚 has/have 否定句的用法：

I （我）	don't	have	dogs.
You （你）	don't	have	cats.
It （牠）	doesn't	have	water.
She （她）	doesn't	have	a computer.
He （他）	doesn't	have	a bike.
We （我們）	don't	have	cars.
You （你們）	don't	have	milk.
They （他們）	don't	have	birds.

＊注意：第三人稱 he, she, it 用 does not，其他用 do not。

另外要注意的是，不管第幾人稱， do not 和 does not 後面的 have 都要用動詞原形 have ，切不可用 has。

例如：

She has a house.

She doesn't have a car.（has 改為否定時，要用原形動詞 have）。

＊注意：be 動詞不可以跟動詞 have 連在一起。

I am have a book.(錯)

I have a book.(對)

7-4

練習題

7-4-1 填充（have/has 否定和肯定）

1.   He_____have a bicycle. He _____ a car.

(他沒有腳踏車。他有一輛車。)

2.   I _____ have a cat. I _____ a dog.

(我沒有一隻貓。我有一隻狗。)

3.   She _____ have a chair. She _____ a desk.

(她沒有一張椅子。她有一張桌子。)

4.   They _____ have pens. They _____ pencils.

(他們沒有筆。他們有鉛筆。)

5.   He _____ have a house. He _____ a car.

(他沒有一幢房子。他有一輛車。)

6.   We _____ have books. We _____ a computer.

(我們沒有書。我們有一台電腦。)

7.   You _____ have students. You _____ teachers.

(你沒有學生。你有老師。)

8.   You _____ have dogs. You _____ cats.

(你們沒有狗。你們有貓。)

9.   She _____ have a mother. She _____ a father.

(她沒有媽媽。她有爸爸。)

10.   He _____ have brothers. He _____ a sister.

(他沒有兄弟。他有一個妹妹。)

7-4-2 改錯

1. I am not（don't）have a dog.
2. She don't have a computer.
3. My brother don't have a bike.
4. They doesn't have cars.
5. We are not have chairs.
6. She isn't have my teacher.
7. It don't have water.
8. He isn't have seven tables.
9. His daughter don't have friends.
10. My brother don't has a car.

7-4-3 英文該怎麼寫？

1. 我沒有一幢房子。

   _____

2. 他沒有鉛筆。

   _____

3. 她沒有學生。

   _____

4. 我們沒有爸爸。

   _____

5. 他們沒有鳥。

   _____

6. 你沒有兄弟。

   _____

7.　　牠沒有朋友。

　　　　_____

8.　　你們沒有女兒。你們有一個兒子。

　　　　_____

9.　　我沒有朋友。我有一隻狗。

　　　　_____

10.　他沒有一台電腦。

　　　　_____

7-4-4　英文該怎麼寫？（混合題）

1.　　他不是我的老師。

　　　　_____

2.　　他沒有學生。

　　　　_____

3.　　我不是學生。

　　　　_____

4.　　我沒有學生。

　　　　_____

5.　　她是醫生。

　　　　_____

6.　　她沒有鉛筆。

　　　　_____

7.　　他們沒有電腦。（computers）

　　　　_____

8.　　我們沒有朋友。

　　　　_____

9.　我是她的朋友。
　　_____

10.　你們有三隻狗。
　　_____

11.　我有五個女兒。
　　_____

12.　他沒有兒子。
　　_____

13.　他是我的老師。
　　_____

14.　他們是我的學生。
　　_____

15.　他不是醫生。
　　_____

第 八 課 （朗讀光碟　第 9 軌）

動詞

除了前一章我們學的動詞 have 和 has 外，英文還有其他許許多多的動詞，該注意的是，第三人稱後面接的動詞要加 <u>s</u>。

例如：She like<u>s</u> Coke. 她喜歡可樂。

8-1　生字

every day	每天
go	去
go to school	上學
read	讀
read books	讀書
eat	吃
eat breakfast	吃早餐
eat lunch	吃午餐
eat dinner	吃晚餐
drink	喝
drink water	喝水
drink milk	喝牛奶
drink Coke	喝可樂
like	喜歡
like cats	喜歡貓
like music	喜歡音樂
like movies	喜歡電影

8-2　課文

I drink water every day.　　　　我每天喝水。

You go to school every day.　　　你每天上學。

She eats breakfast every day.　　她每天吃早餐。

He drinks milk every day.　　　　他每天喝牛奶。

It drinks water every day.　　　　牠每天喝水。

（It可能代表一隻狗，牠每天都喝水）。

We read books every day.　　　　我們每天讀書。

You eat lunch every day.　　　　你們每天吃午餐。

They drink Coke every day.　　　他們每天喝可樂。

He likes movies.　　　　　　　　他喜歡電影。

She likes music.　　　　　　　　她喜歡音樂。

＊有沒有注意到She, He 和 It 後面的動詞都加了 "s"? 因為 She,He,和 It 叫做「第三人稱」，第三人稱後面的動詞要加 "s"。

＊ every day 不能寫成 everyday。 everyday 是形容詞，例如 everyday work （每天的工作）。

8-3　我們看下列圖表：

I	go to school	every day.
You	go to school	every day.
She	goes to school	every day.
He	goes to school	every day.
We	go to school	every day.
You	go to school	every day.
They	go to school	every day.

＊注意：go 是一個比較特別的動詞，用在第三人稱時寫成 "goes"。

 8-4

跟 have 一樣，否定的動詞只要在動詞前加 don't 或 doesn't。請看下列圖表：

I	don't	go to school	every day.
You	don't	go to school	every day.
She	doesn't	go to school	every day.
He	doesn't	go to school	every day.
We	don't	go to school	every day.
You	don't	go to school	every day.
They	don't	go to school	every day.

＊注意：doesn't 後面的動詞都用原形，不用加 s。例如：

He <u>doesn't read</u> books every day.

She <u>doesn't eat</u> breakfast every day.

It <u>doesn't drink</u> water every day.

8-5   練習題

8-5-1 填填看

1.   I _____ her dog.

   （我喜歡她的狗。）

2.   You_____ _____ her dog.

   （你不喜歡她的狗。）

3.   They _____my books.

   （他們喜歡我的書）

4.   You _____ _____ my books.

   （你們不喜歡我的書）

5.   I _____ milk every day.

   （我每天喝牛奶。）

6.   He _____ _____ milk every day.

   （他沒有每天喝牛奶。）

7.   You _____ dogs and cats.

   （你喜歡狗和貓。）

8.   She_____ _____dogs and cats.

   （她不喜歡狗和貓。）

9.   She _____ books every day.

   （她每天讀書。）

10.   He _____ _____ books every day.

   （他沒有每天讀書。）

11. He _____ breakfast every day.

（他每天都吃早餐。）

12. We _____ _____breakfast every day.

（ 我們沒有每天吃早餐。）

13. They _____ Coke every day.

（他們每天都喝可樂。）

14. We _____ _____ Coke every day.

（我們沒有每天都喝可樂。）

15. We _____ to his house every day.

（我們每天都去他家。）

16. We _____ _____to his house every day.

（我們沒有每天都去他家。）

17. He _____ my books.

（他讀我的書。）

18. They _____ _____ my books.

（他們不讀我的書。）

19. We _____ _____ his Coke.

（我們不喝他的可樂。）

20. It _____ _____ my lunch.

（牠不吃我的午餐。）

21. His doctor _____ _____ Coke.

（他的醫生不喝可樂。）

22. Their teacher _____ music.

（他們的老師喜歡音樂。）

23. My dad _____two books every day.

（我的爸爸每天讀兩本書。）

24.   Their sister _____ _____ lunch.

（他們的妹妹不吃午餐。）

25.   He _____Coke.

（他喜歡可樂。）

8-5-2 改錯

1.   He don't like milk.

2.   She like water.

3.   My dog drink water every day.

4.   She don't read my books.

5.   I am not have a dog.

6.   His father do not have a house.

7.   My sister like movies.

8.   His daughter isn't have a dog.

9.   Our cats doesn't like water.

10.   Their son do not have a car.

11.   He doesn't has sisters.

12.   We don't likes music.

13.   Amy's sister do not eat lunch every day.

14.   We reads two books every day.

15.   My daughter doesn't has pencils.

8-5-3 英文該怎麼寫？

1.   我不喜歡鳥（birds）。

_____

2.　他們不喜歡音樂（music）。

　　_____

3.　他們每天喝牛奶（milk）。

　　_____

4.　牠不喝牛奶（milk）。

　　_____

5.　你們每天上學（go to school）。

　　_____

6.　我的老師不吃午餐（lunch）。

　　_____

7.　你們的哥哥喜歡讀書（likes to read books）.

　　_____

8.　他不讀我的書（books）。

　　_____

9.　我的爸爸不喜歡電腦（computers）。

　　_____

10.　她的哥哥不吃早餐（breakfast）。

　　_____

11.　我們不喜歡電影（movies）。

　　_____

12.　他們不喜歡音樂（music）。

　　_____

13.　她不讀她媽媽的書（books）。

　　　＿＿＿＿＿＿＿＿＿＿＿＿＿＿＿＿＿＿＿

14.　我們的兒子不喝可樂（Coke）。

　　　＿＿＿＿＿＿＿＿＿＿＿＿＿＿＿＿＿＿＿

15.　你們每天不吃晚餐（dinner）。

　　　＿＿＿＿＿＿＿＿＿＿＿＿＿＿＿＿＿＿＿

第九課　　　（朗讀光碟　第 10 軌）

問句
（be 動詞問句）

我們用英文問別人問題時所用的特殊句型叫做「問句」，現在我們先介紹「be 動詞的問句」，例如：Is he your father？（他是不是你的爸爸？）

9-1　生字

yes	是，對
no	不是，不對
or	或
engineer	工程師
happy	快樂
sad	悲傷
small	小
big	大

9-2 課文

Are you an engineer？	你是工程師嗎？

（＊注意：engineer 的第一個字母發音是母音，所以 a 要改為 an）

Yes, I am.	是的，我是。
Is your father a doctor？	你的父親是醫生嗎？

（＊注意：your father 是第三人稱 he，所以要用 Is 來問。）

No, he isn't . He's a teacher.	不，他不是。他是一個老師。
Are you happy？	你高興嗎？
No, I am not. I am sad.	不，我不高興，我很難過。
Are they big？	他們很大嗎？
No, they aren't. They're small.	不，他們不大，他們很小。
Are you an engineer or a doctor?	你是工程師還是醫生？
I'm an engineer.	我是工程師。
Is your dog big or small?	你的狗大還是小？
It's big.	牠很大。

9-3　be 動詞問句

・請看下面 be 動詞問句的一個例句：

Is he your father？（他是不是你的爸爸）？

你的回答可能有兩種：

Yes, he is.（是的，他是。）或 No, he isn't .（ 不是，他不是）。

・有時候我們會用「或」的問句：

例如：Is she a doctor or a nurse？（她是醫生還是護士？）

你的回答也可能有兩種：She is a doctor. 或 She is a nurse.

・你也許已經發現，be動詞的問句很簡單，只要把be動詞跟前面的主詞對調即可。例如：She is a teacher. 問句：Is she a teacher？

 ## 9-3-1　yes/no　的問句及回答

Are	you	a teacher ?	Yes,	I am.
Is	he	a student ?	No,	he isn't.
Is	she	happy ?	Yes,	she is.
Is	it	small ?	No,	it isn't.
Are	you	his sons ?	Yes,	we are.
Are	they	your brothers ?	No,	they aren't.

 ## 9-3-2　or 的問句及回答

Are	you	a teacher	or	a student ?	I'm a student.
Is	he	a singer	or	an actor ?	He's an actor.
Is	she	a happy	or	a sad mother ?	She's a happy mother.
Is	it	a small bird	or	a big bird ?	It's a small bird.
Are	you	his sons	or	her sons ?	We're her sons.
Are	they	your computers	or	our computers ?	They're your computers.

9-4-1　填充

1. _____ they your brothers?

2. _____ he your teacher or her teacher?

3. _____ she her mother or his mother?

4. _____ they happy or sad?

5. _____ you an engineer?

6. _____ it a big cat?

7. _____ they small houses?

8. _____ you a happy mother?

9. _____ she an engineer or a doctor?

10. _____ he your son?

11. _____ they your sisters?

12. _____ your sister a student?

13. _____ your brothers teachers?

14. _____his dog a big dog?

15. _____ her mother a doctor?

9-4-2　問答

1. Are you a happy student?

   No, _____

2. Is he your friend?

   Yes, _____

3.   Is she your sister?

No, _____

4.   Are they friends?

Yes, _____

5.   Is she your teacher?

No, _____

6.   Are they your students?

Yes, _____.

7.   Is he your friend or her friend?

_____ her friend.

8.   Are they singers or actors.

_____ singers.

9.   Is your chair big or small?

_____ big.

10.   Is your mother an engineer or a doctor?

_____ an engineer.

11.   Are your teachers happy or sad?

_____ happy.

12.   Is your brother a singer or an actor?

_____ a singer.

13.   Is your sister a happy doctor?

Yes, _____

14.   Is your mom a happy mother?

Yes, _____

15.   Are their sons students?

Yes, _____

9-4-3　改錯

1.　Are（Is）your mom a teacher?

2.　Is your brothers engineers?

3.　Are their son a student?

4.　Are their daughter a singer?

5.　Is your students singers or actors?

6.　Are your father a teacher or an actor?

7.　Is your dogs big or small?

8.　Are your daughter a student or a teacher?

9.　Is his sons actors?

10.　Are your cat small?

11.　Do your mom a doctor?

12.　Does the girl your student?

13.　Does he happy?

14.　Does your dog big?

15.　Do they happy?

第十課 （朗讀光碟 第 11 軌）

問句
（動詞問句）

動詞的問句只需在動詞前面加 Do 或 Does，句尾加問號「？」即可。注意，he, she, it 前面用 Does，其他都用 Do。

Do you like fish ?

10-1 生字

cake	蛋糕
fish	魚
this	這個
that	那個
take a shower	洗澡（淋浴）
take a nap	睡午覺
do homework	做功課

10-2 課文

Do you like this cake?	你喜歡這個蛋糕嗎？
Yes, I do.	是的，我喜歡。
Does she like fish?	她喜歡魚嗎？
No, she doesn't.	不，她不喜歡。
Does he like this cake or that cake?	
	他喜歡這個蛋糕還是那個蛋糕？
He likes that cake.	他喜歡那個蛋糕。
Does your cat take a nap?	你的貓睡午覺嗎？
No, it doesn't.	不，牠不睡。
Do you take a shower every day?	
	你們每天洗澡嗎？
Yes, we do.	是，我們洗。
Do they do their homework every day?	
	他們每天都寫功課嗎？
Yes, they do.	對，他們做。

10-3-1　yes/no 的問句及簡答

Do	you	like this book?	Yes,	I do.
Does	he	like that desk?	No,	he doesn't.
Does	she	have daughters?	Yes,	she does.
Does	it	like this fish?	No,	it doesn't.
Do	you	have pencils?	Yes,	we do.
Do	they	have brothers?	No,	they don't.

＊ Do 和 Does 後面動詞都用原形，即使第三人稱也不加 "s"

 10-3-2　or 的問句及回答

Do	you	like this book	or	that book?	I like that book.
Does	he	like this desk	or	that desk?	He likes this desk.
Does	she	have sons	or	daughters?	She has sons.
Does	it	like this fish	or	that fish?	It likes that fish.
Do	you	have pens	or	pencils?	We have pencils.
Do	they	have brothers	or	sisters?	They have brothers.

10-4-1 填填看

1. _____ you eat fish?

2. _____ he have brothers?

3. _____ it take a nap every day?

4. _____ your mom have a computer?

5. _____ her sister have birds?

6. _____ his brother eat lunch or dinner?

7. _____ they like this cake or that cake?

8. _____ your dad take a shower every day?

9. _____ his teacher take a nap every day?

10. _____ she do her homework every day?

11. _____ she like this singer or that singer?

12. _____ they like this computer or that one?

13. _____ your daughter have a computer?

14. _____ his son do his homework every day?

15. _____ you drink milk or water?

10-4-2 問答：

1. Does he like cats?

   No, _____

2. Do they like cakes?

   Yes, _____

3. Does she like birds or cats?

   She _____

4. Do your sisters like this movie?

   Yes, _____

5. Does your mom like music?

   Yes, _____

6. Does your daughter have a computer?

   Yes, _____

7. Do your students go to school every day?

   Yes, _____

8. Do their cats like fish?

   Yes, _____

9. Do you like this doctor or that doctor?

   I _____

10. Does their teacher eat breakfast every day?

    Yes, _____

11. Do you like this cake or that cake?

    I _____

12. Do they like this movie or that movie?

    They _____

13. Does their son have a computer?

    Yes, _____

14. Do their teachers drink Coke?

    No, _____

15. Does his dog have a big house?

    No, _____

10-4-3　改錯

1.　Do（Does）your daughter like fish?

2.　Does your brothers like this cake?

3.　Does he takes a shower every day?

4.　Does your mom and dad eat breakfast every day?

5.　Does his dog and cat drink milk?

6.　Does your son takes a nap every day?

7.　Do their daughter like this fish or that fish?

8.　Is she go to school every day?

9.　Does they like pencils or pens?

10.　Is their mom drink Coke?

11.　Does that doctor likes music?

12.　Does your cats big or small?

13.　Does your nurse takes a nap?

14.　Does he likes cakes?

15.　Do she eat fish?

10-4-4　英文該怎麼寫？

1.　她有一隻大狗嗎？

_____

2.　你有很多書嗎？（many）

_____

3.　他們有四棟大房子嗎？

_____

4.　你們喜歡這個女孩嗎？

_____

5. 你的媽媽喜歡這塊蛋糕嗎？

　　_____

6. 他的爸爸每天都睡午覺嗎？

　　_____

7. 她的女兒每天都上學嗎？

　　_____

8. 這位護士每天都讀書嗎？

　　_____

9. 那位醫生每天都高興嗎？

　　_____

10. 你的貓每天吃魚嗎？

　　_____

11. 那個男孩每天喝牛奶嗎？

　　_____

12. 你的學生們每天吃早餐嗎？

　　_____

13. 你們的兒子喝可樂還是水？

　　_____

14. 你的哥哥每天做功課嗎？（do his homework）

　　_____

15. Amy 喜歡音樂嗎？

　　_____

第十一課 （朗讀光碟 第 12 軌）

問句
（Wh 型問句）

Wh 型的問句需要回答的人提供確切的答案，例如：

Where do you live? 你住在哪裡？

I live in Tainan. 我住在台南。

Where do you live?

who	誰
what	什麼
when	什麼時候
how	如何
where	哪裡
which	哪一個
at	在（介系詞）
by	搭乘（介系詞）
in	在（介系詞）

11-2　課文

Who are they?	他們是誰？
They're my students.	他們是我的學生。
What does he do?	他做什麼的？
He's a teacher.	他是老師。
When does she go to school?	她什麼時候上學？
She goes to school at 7:00 A.M.	她上午七點上學。

＊上午用 A.M.表示，中午以後用 P.M.表示。在幾點鐘時要用 at 。

How does she go to school?	她怎麼去學校？
She goes to school by bus.	她搭巴士去上學。

＊搭乘交通工具用 by

Where is their school?	他們的學校在哪裡？
Their school is in Taichung.	他們的學校在台中。

＊在什麼城市用 in

Which book is his?	哪一本書是他的？
This one.	這一本。

How do you like this book?　　你覺得這本書如何？

I don't like it.　　　　　　　我不喜歡。

＊注意：Where（哪裡）、Who（誰）、When（什麼時候）、How（如何）、 Which（哪一個）、 What（什麼） 後面直接接 be 動詞或動詞問句。

11-3　練習題

11-3-1　選選看

1. （　　）（1）Where　（2）How　（3）Who　is your mom?
   She is in Taichung.

2. （　　）（1）Who　（2）How　（3）Where　are your brothers?
   They are at home.（在家）

3. （　　）（1）What　（2）How　（3）Which　does your mother do?
   She's a doctor.

4. （　　）（1）Where　（2）How　（3）Who do you like this movie?
   I don't like it.

5. （　　）（1）Which　（2）How　（3）Who birds do you like?
   I like this one.

6. （　　）（1）Where　（2）What　（3）Who is that?
   That is a pencil.

7. （　　）（1）Where　（2）How　（3）Who is your dad?
   He's fine.（很好）

8. （　　）（1）Where　（2）How　（3）What　do you like?
   I like this pen.

9. （　　）（1）Where　（2）When　（3）Who does he take a nap?
   He takes a nap at 2:00 P.M.

10. （　　）（1）Which　（2）How　（3）Who house is your house?
    That one.

11. （　　）（1）Where　（2）How　（3）When do you do your homework?
    I do my homework at 8:00 P.M.

12. （　　）（1）What　（2）How　（3）Who　do you drink every day?

　　　I drink milk and water.

13. （　　）（1）Where　（2）How　（3）Who　is your computer?

　　　It's in the house.

14. （　　）（1）Where　（2）How　（3）Who　is that girl?

　　　She's my sister.

15. （　　）（1）Where　（2）How　（3）Who　is that boy?

　　　He's my friend.

11-3-2 填填看（when, who, where, how, what, which）

1. _____ do you eat breakfast?

　　I eat breakfast at home.（我在家吃早餐。）

2. _____ does she eat lunch?

　　She eats lunch at 12:00A.M.

3. _____ does your son go to school ?

　　He goes to school at 7A.M.

4. _____ does your daughter go to school?

　　She goes to school by bus.

5. _____ is my book?

　　It's in your house.

6. _____ are my cats?

　　They are in your school.

7. _____ is your sister?（誰是你的姊姊？）

　　Amy is my sister.

8. _____ does your sister do?

　　She's a doctor.

9. _____ does he like this book?

He doesn't like it.

10. _____ are my dogs? They are in his house.

11. _____is this? This is a cat.

12. _____ does your mom do? She is an engineer.

13. _____ cat is your cat? That one.（那隻。）

14. _____ book do you like? I like that book.

15. _____ is your friend? Amy is my friend.

11-3-3 英文該怎麼寫？

1. 這是什麼？

   _____

2. 你的貓在哪裡？

   _____

3. 你喜歡哪一本書？

   _____

4. 你住在哪裡？

   _____

5. 你什麼時候上學？

   _____

6. 你怎麼去學校？

   _____

7. 誰是你爸爸的醫生？

   _____

8.　　你是做什麼的？（你的職業是什麼？）

_____

9.　　你每天什麼時候洗澡？

_____

10.　你的爸爸媽媽如何？（你的爸爸媽媽好嗎？）

_____

第十二課 （朗讀光碟 第13軌）

現在式和現在進行式

「現在式」是用經常做的事、已成為習慣的事，還有不變的事實或真理。至於你現在正在做的事，反倒不能用「現在式」，要用「現在進行式」。

I'm eating lunch now.

now	現在
play computer games	玩電腦遊戲
（遊戲不只一種，所以 game 要加 s）	
listen to music	聽音樂
watch TV	看電視
call friends	打電話給朋友

12-2　課文

I'm watching TV now.（現在進行式）

我現在正在看電視。

I watch TV every day.（現在式）

我每天看電視。

You're playing computer games now.（現在進行式）

你現在正在玩電腦遊戲。

You don't play computer games every day.（現在式）

你沒有每天玩電腦遊戲。

She's taking a shower now.（現在進行式）

她現在正在洗澡。

She takes a shower every day.（現在式）

她每天洗澡。

He's doing his homework now.（現在進行式）

他現在正在做功課。

He does homework every day.（現在式）

他每天做功課。

It's taking a nap.（現在進行式）

牠正在睡午覺。

It takes a nap every day.（現在式）

牠每天睡午覺。

We're calling our friends now.（現在進行式）

我們現在正在打電話給我們的朋友。

We call our friends every day.（現在式）

我們每天打電話給朋友。

They're listening to music now.（現在進行式）

他們現在正在聽音樂。

They listen to music every day.（現在式）

他們每天聽音樂。

＊注意 take 加 ing 時 e 要去掉：take → taking。

 12-3　請看圖表：

I'm	taking a shower. 正在洗澡
You're	doing homework. 正在做功課
He's	listening to music. 正在聽音樂
She's	calling her friend. 正在打電話給她的朋友
It's	eating fish. 正在吃魚
We're	taking a nap. 正在睡午覺
You're	playing computer games. 正在玩電腦遊戲
They're	watching TV. 正在看電視

＊你還記得嗎？

I'm=I am, You're = You are, He's =He is, She's=She is,It's=It is,
We're=We are, You're=You are, They're=They are

 12-4

如果有人問你每天例行做些什麼事what do you do every day? 這時候你
得用「現在式」來回答：

I go to school every day.

I watch TV every day.

I play computer games every day.

I do my homework every day.

I take a shower every day.

I call my friends every day.

＊注意：如果有人問你 What do you do？是問你的職業，
你可以回答說：I'm a student.

 12-5

如果有人問你現在正在做什麼？

What are you doing now？ 你得用「現在進行式」來回答：

I'm playing computer games.

我正在玩電腦遊戲。

I'm taking a shower.

我正在洗澡。

I'm watching TV.

我正在看電視。

I'm doing my homework.

我正在做功課。

I'm calling my friend.

我正在打電話給我的朋友。

I'm listening to music.

我正在聽音樂。

12-6-1 填填看

＊注意：第三人稱（He, She, It）後面的動詞要加 s

1. He ＿＿＿＿＿＿＿＿＿（do）his homework now.

2. We ＿＿＿＿＿＿＿＿＿（read）books now.

3. My dad ＿＿＿＿＿＿＿＿（take）a shower every day.

4. His sister＿＿＿＿＿＿＿＿（play）computer games every day.

5. Your dog ＿＿＿＿＿＿＿（take a nap）every day.

6. We ＿＿＿＿＿＿（watch）TV every day.

7. Who ＿＿＿＿＿＿＿＿（watch）TV now?

8. What is he ＿＿＿＿＿＿（read）?

9. What do you ＿＿＿＿＿（read）every day?

10. His mom ＿＿＿＿＿＿＿＿（take）a shower now.

11. She ＿＿＿＿＿＿（take）a shower every day.

12. My sister ＿＿＿＿＿＿＿＿（sleep）now.

13. My friend ＿＿＿＿＿＿＿（call）me every day.

14. They ＿＿＿＿＿＿（go）to school now.

15. Does he ＿＿＿＿＿＿（go）to school every day?

16. Your teacher ＿＿＿＿＿＿（listen）to music now.

17. Her friend ＿＿＿＿＿＿＿（listen）to music every day.

18. Who ＿＿＿＿＿＿＿＿（play）computer games now?

19. My sister ＿＿＿＿＿＿＿（play）computer games now.

20. She ＿＿＿＿＿（play）computer games every day.

21.　I _____（eat）breakfast every day.

22.　My friend _____（eat）lunch now.

23.　They _____（watch）TV now.

24.　It _____（watch）a bird now.（我們這裡假設 it 是隻貓）。

25.　Their teacher _____（call）students every day.

12-6-2　問答

1.　What is your mom eating now?

　　_____（cakes）

2.　What is your dad doing now?

　　He _____（play computer games）

3.　What is your cat doing now?

　　It _____（take a nap）

4.　What is your sister reading?

　　She _____（a book）

5.　What are they doing?

　　They _____（watch TV）

6.　What are your mom and dad doing?

　　They_____（read books）

7.　What is your cat watching?

　　It _____（a bird）

8.　What are your brothers playing?

　　They _____（cards 撲克牌）

9.　What are you doing now?

　　I _____（do my homework）

10.   What is that dog doing now?

It _____（take a nap）

11.   What are your friends doing now?

They _____（eat dinner）

12.   What is your teacher doing now?

She _____（read a book）

13.   What is her brother drinking?

He _____（milk）

14.   What are her sisters doing?

They _____（eat breakfast）

15.   What is your dad doing?

He _____（take a shower）

12-6-3　改錯

1.   He go（is going）to school now.

2.   I am watching TV every day.

3.   He take a nap every day.

4.   He is take a nap now.

5.   My mother is take a shower now.

6.   This girl do not like cakes.

7.   That boy are doing homework now.

8.   My brother do not go to school every day.

9.   They are listens to music now.

10.   We are read books now.

12-6-4　英文該怎麼寫

1.　你正在做什麼？

　　_____

2.　我正在打電話給我的媽媽。

　　_____

3.　你是做什麼的？（你的職業是什麼？）

　　_____

4.　我是一個演員。

　　_____

5.　他的護士正在聽音樂。

　　_____

6.　我們的女兒現在正在看電視。

　　_____

7.　她的兒子現在正在玩電腦遊戲。

　　_____

8.　我每天洗澡。

　　_____

9.　他現在正在洗澡。

　　_____

10.　這個女孩現在正在打電話給她的朋友。

　　_____

上冊總複習

Ⅰ. 選擇題

1. （　）He（1）has（2）have（3）is two sisters.
2. （　）They（1）isn't（2）aren't（3）is my friends.
3. （　）His mom has many（1）friends（2）sister（3）doctor.
4. （　）This girl（1）is（2）does has（3）has a dog.
5. （　）Their daughter（1）take（2）takes（3）is taking a shower every day.
6. （　）Our mom（1）doesn't（2）don't（3）aren't like dogs.
7. （　）（1）Is（2）Do（3）Does this actor like computer games?
8. （　）Her teacher（1）aren't（2）doesn't（3）don't have three houses.
9. （　）When（1）do you（2）are you（3）have you take a nap every day?
10. （　）Where（1）do he（2）is he（3）does he live?
11. （　）Which book does she（1）likes（2）like（3）is like?
12. （　）How（1）does（2）is（3）do your brother go to school?
13. （　）My dad is（1）calls（2）call（3）calling his friend now.
14. （　）How（1）is（2）are（3）do your mom and dad?（你的爸媽好嗎？）
15. （　）Their teacher（1）goes（2）go（3）is go to school every day.
16. （　）What（1）do（2）does（3）is your cat doing?
17. （　）He（1）don't（2）doesn't（3）isn't have a car. He has a bike.
18. （　）My nurse（1）is read（2）reads（3）is reading a book now.
19. （　）This engineer（1）is（2）are（3）does my father's good friend.
20. （　）（1）Does（2）Is（3）Are their sister a doctor?

II. 填充題

1. He _____ have a cat, but he has many dogs.

2. You _____ have a car, but you have a bike.

3. It _____ drink water, but it drinks milk.

4. My friend _____ have brothers, but he has a sister.

5. My teacher doesn't watch TV. He _____ books.（看書）

6. They _____ have pencils, but they have many pens.（沒有）

7. Amy _____ my teacher. She is my sister's teacher.（不是）

8. _____ they your teachers or his teachers?（是）

9. _____ you an engineer? （是）

10. _____ it a big cat? （是）

11. _____ he take a shower every day?

12. _____ you a happy mother?（是）

13. _____ they singers or actors? （是）

14. _____ is that girl? She is at home.（在哪裡？）

15. _____ is your dog doing? It's drinking milk.

16. _____ do you go to school? I go to school by bus.

17. _____ is your mother? She is fine.（很好）

18. _____ does your mother do? She is an engineer.

19. _____ does your mother do every day. She plays basketball.

20. _____ book do you like, this one or that one? I like that one.

III. 問答

1. What is your brother doing?

   He_____ （正在看電視。）

2. Do you take a nap every day?

Yes, _____

3. Do your teachers go to school every day?

No, _____

4. Does your dad have many books?

Yes, _____

5. Are your sisters doctors?

Yes, _____

6. What does your son do?

He _____ （一位歌星）

7. Who is she calling?

She _____ （她的朋友）

8. Does your daughter play computer games every day?

No, _____

9. Do you read books or watch TV every day?

I _____ （看書）

10. Does he do his homework every day?

No, _____

11. Is Amy your mother's doctor?

Yes, _____

12. Which dog do you like?

I _____ （那隻。）

13. Are they your chairs?

No, _____ They are Amy's.

14. Where does your teacher live?

She _____ （Taichung 台中）

15. Do you eat breakfast every day?

    Yes, _____

16. What are they doing now?

    They _____ （正在吃午餐）

17. Do your friends drink Coke?

    No, _____

18. When does she take a nap every day?

    She _____ （at 1:00 P.M.）

19. When do you eat dinner every day?

    I _____ （at 6:00 P.M.）

20. Are you brother and sister?

    No, _____

IV.　改錯

1. She don't（doesn't）like computer games.

2. I not like computer games.

3. My dad isn't have a car.

4. His doctor don't drink Coke.

5. What do she do?

6. She is engineer.

7. They are eat dinner now.

8. His daughter is not live at home.

9. My mom and dad doesn't eat lunch.

10. Her sisters are my student.

11. My mom have many books.

12. They have many daughter.

13. How is your mom and dad?

14. Which book do she like?

15. When does he goes to school every day?

16. This engineer is watch TV now.

17. His cat is drink milk every day.

18. She doesn't has friends.

19. I take a shower now.

20. Does your brother and sister eat breakfast every day?

V. 英文該怎麼寫？

1. 我不是他的老師。

   _____

2. 他不是我的學生。

   _____

3. 他的姊姊每天玩電腦遊戲。

   _____

4. 這個男孩正在看電視。

   _____

5. 她是做什麼的？（她的職業是什麼？）

   _____

6. 她是一位工程師。

   _____

7. 我的弟弟正在聽音樂。

   _____

8. 他不喜歡這張書桌。

   _____

9.　我的爸爸不喜歡那把椅子。

　　_____

10.　我老師的妹妹有很多書。

　　_____

11.　她是一位工程師還是一位醫生？

　　_____

12.　他每天怎麼上學？（搭乘什麼交通工具？）

　　_____

13.　他都騎腳踏車上學。

　　_____

14.　他們的妹妹每天都不吃午餐。

　　_____

15.　我每天晚上九點洗澡。（at 9:00P.M.）

　　_____

16.　Amy 是誰？

　　_____

17.　Amy 是我哥哥的朋友。

　　_____

18.　哪一個女孩是你的學生？（Which girl）

　　_____

19.　你現在正在打電話給你的媽媽嗎？

　　_____

20.　她有九隻大狗。

　　_____

習題解答

第一課 家人

1-3-1 選選看

1.（3）2.（2）3.（1）4.（3）5.（1）6.（2）7.（1）8.（2）

1-3-2 下面的字，英文該怎麼寫：

1.boy　2.brother　3.sister　4.father　5.brother　6.sister　7.mother　8.girl

9.a mother and a father　10. a sister and a brother　11.a daughter and a son

12.a mother and a sister　13.a father and a sister　14.a brother and a sister

15.a girl and a boy

第二課 你、我、他

2-3-1 填填看

1.（am）2.（is）3.（is）4.（is）5.（are）6.（are）7.（are）8.（are）9.（are）10.（are）

11.（are）12.（are）13.（are）14.（are）15.（are）

2-3-2　英文該怎麼寫？

1. We're friends.　2. He's the brother.　3. I'm the sister.　4. They're brother and sister.

5. He's the father.　6. He's the son.　7. They're father and son.　8. She's the mother.

9. I'm the daughter.　10. We're mother and daughter.　11. She's the sister.　12.
You're sisters.　13. They're a dog and a cat.　14. They're boys and girls.　15.
You're daughters.

第三課 有

3-3-1 選選看

1.（1）2.（4）3.（3）4.（1）5.（1）6.（3）7.（4）8.（1）9.（4）10.（1）

3-3-2 填填看

1.（have）2.（has）3.（have）4.（are）5.（have）6.（has）7.（is）8.（are）9.（have）10.（have）11.（are）12.（has）13.（are）14.（have）15.（have）16.（has）17.（have）18.（are）19.（are）20.（have）

3-3-3 改錯

1.（has→have）2.（has→have）3.（have→has）4.（has→have）5.（has→have）6.（have→has）7.（has→have）8.（has→have）9.（have→has）10.（have→has）11.（去are）12.（cat→cats）13.（book→a book）14.（去are）15.（去is）.

第四課 數字

4-2-1　現在把次序打亂，你能填得出正確的數字來嗎？
3,2,5,0,7,10,1,4,6,8,9

4-3-1 選選看
1.（1）2.（2）3.（3）4.（1）5.（2）6（2）7.（1）8.（2）9.（1）10.（2）11.（1）12.（3）13.（1）14.（2）15.（1）

4-3-2 填填看
1.five boys　2.seven girls　3.three sons　4.eight desks　5.one brother　6.six books　7.two sisters　8.four cats　9. ten chairs　10.nine dogs　11.five sisters　12.two teachers　13.one daughter　14.three dogs　15.eight houses

4-3-3 英文該怎麼寫？
1.I have five cats.　2.He has three dogs.　3.We have four chairs.　4.They have one desk.　5.She has two houses.　6.I have ten students.　7.He has many books.

8.You have three friends.　9.You have two teachers.　10.We have nine chairs.

第五課 所有格——我的、你的、他的

5-3-1 塡塡看

1.（His）2.（Her）3.（My）4.（His）5.（Their）6.（Your）7.（My）8.（His）9.（Our）10.（Their）11.（My）12.（My, has）13.（Their, have）14.（Their, have）15.（His, has）

5-3-2 改錯

1.（have→has）2.（are→is）3.（is→are）4.（have→has）5.（has→have）6.（is→are）7.（去is）8.（are→is）9.（去is）10.（have→has）11.（has→have）12.（book→books）13.（teacher→a teacher）14.（have→has）15.（去are）

5-3-3 英文該怎麼寫？

1.（I'm his student.）2.（He's my dad.）3.（Amy is my sister.）4.（Amy has a sister.）5.（My teacher has three dogs.）6.（Her friend has many cats.）7.（They're my students.）8.（He has many students.）9.（My daughter has many books.）10.（Their son is my friend.）

第六課 肯定和否定（是、不是）

6-3-1 塡充

1.（am not）2.（isn't）3.（isn't）4.（aren't）5.（isn't）6.（aren't）7.（aren't）8.（aren't）9.（aren't）10.（isn't）11.（isn't）12.（aren't）13.（am not）14.（aren't）15.（aren't）16.（isn't）17.（isn't）18.（isn't）19.（isn't）20.（aren't）21.（aren't）22.（isn't）23.（isn't）24.（aren't）25.（isn't）

6-3-2 改錯

1.（teachers→teacher）2.（isn't→aren't）3.（aren't→isn't）4.（aren't→isn't）

5.（friends→friend） 6.（student→students） 7.（friend→friends） 8.（aren't→isn't） 9.（dogs→dog） 10.（isn't→aren't） 11.（aren't→isn't） 12.（teachers→teacher） 13.（actor→an actor） 14.（pencil→a pencil） 15.（pen→pens）

6-3-3　英文該怎麼寫？

1.（He isn't my mom's student.） 2.（We aren't her daughters.） 3.（It isn't her dog.） 4.（It isn't my chair.） 5.（You aren't my students.） 6.（We aren't her teachers.） 7.（It isn't my cat.） 8.（Amy isn't my daughter.） 9.（We aren't their friends.） 10.（They aren't our desks and chairs.）

第七課 肯定和否定（有、沒有）

7-4-1 填充

1.（doesn't has） 2.（don't have） 3.（doesn't has） 4.（don't have） 5.（doesn't has） 6.（don't have） 7.（don't have） 8.（don't have） 9.（doesn't has） 10.（doesn't has）

7-4-2 改錯

1.（am not→don't） 2.（don't→doesn't） 3.（don't→doesn't） 4.（doesn't→don't） 5.（are not→don't） 6.（去 have） 7.（don't→doesn't） 8.（isn't→doesn't） 9.（don't→doesn't） 10.（don't has→doesn't have）

7-4-3　英文該怎麼寫？

1.（I don't have a house.） 2.（He doesn't have pencils.） 3.（She doesn't have students.） 4.（We don't have fathers.） 5.（They don't have birds.） 6.（You don't have brothers.） 7.（It doesn't have friends.） 8.（You don't have daughters. You have a son.） 9.（I don't have friends. I have a dog.） 10.（He doesn't have a computer.）

7-4-4 英文該怎麼寫？（混合題）

1.（He is not my teacher.）2.（He doesn't have students.）3.（I'm not a student.）4.（I don't have students.）5.（She is a doctor.）6.（She doesn't have pencils.）7.（They don't have computers.）8.（We don't have friends.）9.（I'm her friend.）10.（You have three dogs.）11.（I have five daughters.）12.（He doesn't have sons.）13.（He is my teacher.）14.（They're my students.）15.（He isn't a doctor.）

第八課 動詞

8-5-1 填填看

1.（like）2.（don't like）3.（like）4.（don't like）5.（drink）6.（doesn't drink）7.（like）8.（doesn't like）9.（reads）10.（doesn't read）11.（eats）12.（don't eat）13.（drink）14.（don't drink）15.（go）16.（don't go）17.（reads）18.（don't read）19.（don't drink）20.（doesn't eat）21.（doesn't drink）22.（likes）23.（reads）24.（doesn't eat）25.（likes）

8-5-2 改錯

1.（don't→doesn't）2.（like→likes）3.（drink→drinks）4.（don't→doesn't）5.（am not→don't）6.（do not→doesn't）7.（like→likes）8.（isn't→doesn't）9.（doesn't→don't）10.（do not→doesn't）11.（has→have）12.（likes→like）13.（do not→doesn't）14.（reads→read）15.（has→have）

8-5-3 英文該怎麼寫？

1.（I don't like birds.）2.（They don't like music.）3.（They drink milk every day.）4.（It doesn't drink milk.）5.（You go to school every day.）6.（My teacher doesn't eat lunch.）7.（Your brother likes to read books.）8.（He doesn't read my books.）9.（My father doesn't like computers.）10.（Her brother doesn't eat breakfast.）11.（We don't like movies.）12.（They don't like music.）13.（She doesn't read her mother's book.) 14.(Our son doesn't drink Coke.) 15.(You don't eat dinner every day.)

第九課　問句（be 動詞問句）

9-4-1 填充

1.(Are) 2.(Is) 3.(Is) 4.(Are) 5.(Are) 6.(Is) 7.(Are) 8.(Are) 9.(Is) 10.(Is) 11.(Are) 12.(Is) 13.(Are) 14.(Is) 15.(Is)

9-4-2　問答

1.(I am not.) 2.(he is.) 3.(she isn't.) 4.(they are.) 5.(she isn't.) 6.(they are.) 7.(He is) 8.(They are) 9.(It is) 10.(She is) 11.(They are) 12.(He is) 13.(she is.) 14.(she is.) 15.(they are.)

9-4-3 改錯

1.(Are→Is) 2.(Is→Are) 3.(Are→Is) 4.(Are→Is) 5.(Is→Are) 6.(Are→Is) 7.(Is→Are) 8.(Are→Is) 9.(Is→Are) 10.(Are→Is) 11.(Do→Is) 12.(Does→Is) 13.(Does→Is) 14.(Does→Is) 15.(Do→Are)

第十課　問句（動詞問句）

10-4-1 填填看

1.(Do) 2.(Does) 3.(Does) 4.(Does) 5.(Does) 6.(Does) 7.(Do) 8.(Does) 9.(Does) 10.(Does) 11.(Does) 12.(Do) 13.(Does) 14.(Does) 15.(Do)

10-4-2　問答：

1.(he doesn't.) 2.(they do.) 3.(likes birds(cats.)) 4.(they do.) 5.(she does.) 6.(she does.) 7.(they do.) 8.(they do.) 9.(like this doctor(that doctor.)) 10.(she does.) 11.(like this cake(that cake.)) 12.(like this movie(that movie.)) 13.(he does.) 14.(they don't.) 15.(it doesn't.)

10-4-3 改錯

1.（Do→Does）2.（Does→Do）3.（takes→take）4.（Does→Do）5.（Does →Do）6.（takes→take）7.（Do→Does）8.（Is→Does）9.（Does→Do）10.（Is→Does）11.（likes→like）12.（Does→Are）13.（takes→take）14.（likes →like）15.（Do→Does）

10-4-4 英文該怎麼寫？

1.（Does she have a big dog?）2.（Do you have many books?）3.（Do they have four big houses?）4.（Do you like this girl?）5.（Does your mom like this cake?）6.（Does his dad take a nap every day?）7.（Does her daughter go to school every day?）8.（Does this nurse read books every day?）9.（Is that doctor happy every day?）10.（Does your cat eat fish every day?）11.（Does that boy drink milk every day?）12.（Do your students eat breakfast every day?）13.（Does your son drink Coke or water?）14.（Does your brother do his homework every day?）15.（Does Amy like music?）

第十一課　問句（Wh 型的問句）

11-3-1 選選看

1.（1）2.（3）3.（1）4.（2）5.（1）6.（2）7.（2）8.（3）9.（2）10.（1）11.（3）12.（1）13.（1）14.（3）15.（3）

11-3-2　填填看

1.（Where）2.（When）3.（When）4.（How）5.（Where）6（Where）7.（Who）8.（What）9.（How）10.（Where）11.（What）12.（What）13.（Which）14.（Which）15.（Who）

11-3-3 英文該怎麼寫？

1.（What is this?）2.（Where is your cat?）3.（Which book do you like?）4.（Where do you live?) 5.(When do you go to school?) 6.(How do you go to school?) 7. (Who is your father's doctor?) 8.(What do you do?) 9.(When do you take a shower every day?) 10.(How are your dad and mom?)

第十二課　現在式和現在進行式

12-6-1 填填看

1.(is doing) 2.(are reading) 3.(takes) 4.(plays) 5.(takes a nap) 6.(watch) 7. (is watching) 8.(reading) 9.(read) 10.(is taking) 11.(takes) 12.(is sleeping) 13.(calls) 14.(are going) 15.(go) 16.(is listening) 17.(listens) 18.(is playing) 19.(is playing) 20.(plays) 21.(eat) 22.(is eating) 23.(are watching) 24.(is watching) 25.(calls)

12-6-2　問答

1.(she is eating cakes.) 2.(is playing computer games.) 3.(is taking a nap.) 4.(is reading a book.) 5.(are watching TV.) 6.(are reading books.) 7.(is watching a bird.) 8.(are playing cards.) 9.(am doing my homework.) 10.(is taking a nap.) 11.(are eating dinner.) 12.(is reading a book.) 13.(is drinking milk.) 14.(are eating breakfast.) 15.(is taking a shower.)

12-6-3 改錯

1.(go → is going)　2.(am watching → watch)　3.(take → takes)　4.(take → taking) 5.(take→taking) 6.(do→does) 7.(are→is) 8.(do→does) 9.(listen →listening)　10.(read→reading)

12-6-4 英文該怎麼寫？

1.(What are you doing?) 2.(I am calling my mom.) 3.(What do you do?) 4.(I'm an actor.) 5.(His nurse is listening to music.) 6.(Our daughter is watching TV now.) 7.(Her son is playing computer games now.) 8.(I take a shower every day.) 9.(He's taking a shower now.) 10.(This girl is calling her friend now.)

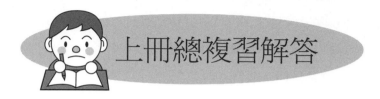上冊總複習解答

I. 選擇題

1.（1）2.（2）3.（1）4.（3）5.（2）6（1）7.（3）8.（2）9.（1）10.（3）11.（2）12.（1）
13.（3）14.（2）15.（1）16（3）17.（2）18.（3）19.（1）20.（2）

II. 填充題

1. doesn't   2. don't   3. doesn't   4. doesn't   5. reads   6. don't   7. isn't   8.
Are   9. Are   10. Is   11. Does   12. Are   13. Are   14. Where   15. What
16. How   17. How   18. What   19. What   20. Which

III. 問答

1. is watching TV.   2. I do.   3.they don't.   4.he does.   5.they are.   6.is a
singer.   7.is calling her friend.   8.she doesn't.   9.read books.   10.he doesn't
11.she is.   12. like that dog（one）.   13.they aren't.   14.lives in Taichung.
15.I do.   16. are eating lunch.   17.they don't.   18.takes a nap at 1:00P.M..
19.eat dinner at 6:00P.M.   20.we are not.

IV. 改錯

1. don't→doesn't   2.not→don't   3.isn't→doesn't   4.don't→doesn't   5.
do→does   6.engineer→an engineer   7.eat→eating   8.is→does 或 live
→living   9.doesn't→don't   10.student→students   11.have→has   12.
daughter→daughters   13.is→are   14.do→does   15.goes→go   16.
watch→watching   17.is drink→drinks   18.has→have   19.take→am

taking　　20.Does → Do

V.　英文該怎麼寫？

1.I am not his teacher.　2.He isn't my student.　3.His sister plays computer games every day.　4. This boy is watching TV.　5.What does she do?　6. She's an engineer.　7.My brother is listening to music.　8.He doesn't like this desk. 9.My dad doesn't like that chair.　10.My teacher's sister has many books.　11. Is she an engineer or a doctor?　12.How does he go to school?　13.He goes to school by bicycle（bike）.　14.Their sister doesn't eat lunch every day. 或 Their sisters don't eat lunch every day.　15.I take a shower at 9:00P.M. every day.　16.Who is Amy?　17.Amy is my brother's friend.　18.Which girl is your student?　19.Are you calling your mom now?　20.She has nine big dogs.

專門替中國人寫的英文課本 初級本（上冊）

2022年4月四版　　　　　　　　　　　　　　　定價：新臺幣250元
有著作權‧翻印必究
Printed in Taiwan.

著　　　　者	文	庭	澍
策 劃 審 訂	李	家	同
責 任 編 輯	何	采	嬪
校　　　對	楊	蕙	芩
整 體 設 計	陳	玉	嵐

出　版　者	聯經出版事業股份有限公司	副 總 編 輯	陳	逸	華
地　　　址	新北市汐止區大同路一段369號1樓	總　編　輯	涂	豐	恩
叢書主編電話	（02）86925588轉5305	總　經　理	陳	芝	宇
台北聯經書房	台北市新生南路三段94號	社　　　長	羅	國	俊
電　　　話	（02）23620308	發　行　人	林	載	爵
台中分公司	台中市北區崇德路一段198號				
暨門市電話	（04）22312023				
郵政劃撥帳戶第0100559-3號					
郵撥電話	（02）23620308				
印　刷　者	世和印製企業有限公司				
總　經　銷	聯合發行股份有限公司				
發　行　所	新北市新店區寶橋路235巷6弄6號2F				
電　　　話	（02）29178022				

行政院新聞局出版事業登記證局版臺業字第0130號

本書如有缺頁，破損，倒裝請寄回台北聯經書房更換。　　ISBN　978-957-08-6267-6 (平裝)
聯經網址 http://www.linkingbooks.com.tw
電子信箱 e-mail:linking@udngroup.com

國家圖書館出版品預行編目資料

專門替中國人寫的英文課本 初級本（上冊）
／文庭澍著 . 四版 . 新北市 . 聯經 . 2022.04
120 面 . 19×26 公分 .
ISBN　978-957-08-6267-6 (平裝附光碟片)
[2022年4月四版]

1. CST：英語　2. CST：讀本

805.18　　　　　　　　　　　　　　111004120

從國人的需求出發的英文學習書

從中國人的需要出發的英文課本

破除現有英文課本的共同缺點　回歸學習英文的基本課程

初級本（上、下冊）

高級本（上冊）

中級本（上、下冊）

聯經出版事業公司
www.linkingbooks.com.tw

郵政劃撥帳號：01005593　戶名：聯經出版事業公司
洽詢電話：02-2641-8662

從國人的需求出發的英文學習書

糾正中國人最容易犯錯的基本文法

專門替中國人寫的
英文基本文法

李家同、海柏◎ 合著

如果你覺得，坊間的文法書太難了：讀完後文法還是不好；如果你真的想打下深厚的文法基礎，可是卻苦無門路，那麼，這本書就適合你。因為這本書是針對中國人最容易犯的文法錯誤所編寫的書！

我們兩人都有過教初級英文的經驗，我們發現我們中國人寫英文句子時，會犯獨特的錯誤，比方說，我們常將兩個動詞連在一起用，我們也會將動詞用成名詞，我們對過去式和現在式毫無觀念。更加不要說現在完成式了。而天生講英文的人是不可能犯這種錯的。

我們這本英文文法書，是專門為中國人寫的。以下是這本書的一些特徵：我們一開始就強調一些英文文法的基本規定，這些規定都是我們中國人所不太習慣的。也就是說，我們一開始就告訴了讀者，大家不要犯這種錯誤。

我們馬上就進入動詞，理由很簡單，這是我們中國人最弱的地方。根據我們的經驗，絕大多數的錯誤，都與動詞有關。這也難怪，中文裡面，哪有什麼動詞的規則？

最後我們要勸告初學的讀者，你們應該多多做練習，練習做多了，你自然不會犯錯。總有一天，你說英文的時候，動詞該加s，你就會加s。該用過去式，就會用過去式。兩個動詞也不會連在一起用，疑問句也會用疑問句的語法。那是多麼美好的一天。希望這一天早日到來！

李家同
海　柏

聯經出版事業公司
www.linkingbooks.com.tw

郵政劃撥帳號：01005593　戶名：聯經出版事業公司
洽詢電話：02-2641-8662

創意十足的英文教學指南